for Andrew and Jack

—J.E.S.

to Luisa and Ricardo

—L.E.

All rights reserved. Published in the United States by Random House Studio,
an imprint of Random House Children's Books, a division of Penguin Random House LLC, New York.
Random House Studio and the colophon are trademarks of Penguin Random House LLC.

Visit us on the Web! rhcbooks.com
Educators and librarians, for a variety of teaching tools, visit us at RHTeachersLibrarians.com

Library of Congress Cataloging-in-Publication Data
Names: Smith, Jennifer E., author. | Espinosa, Leo, illustrator.
Title: The creature of Habit / Jennifer E. Smith ; [illustrated by] Leo Espinosa.
Description: New York : Random House Children's Books, 2021. | Audience: Ages 3–7. | Summary: On the island of Habit
lives a very big creature who does the exact same things in the exact same order every day, but when a small creature comes
along who wants to do something different every day, the creature of Habit must learn to adapt.
Identifiers: LCCN 2020050030 (print) | LCCN 2020050031 (ebook) | ISBN 978-0-593-17305-3 (hardcover)
ISBN 978-0-593-17306-0 (lib. bdg.) | ISBN 978-0-593-17307-7 (ebook)
Subjects: CYAC: Habit—Fiction. | Adaptability (Psychology)—Fiction.
Classification: LCC PZ7.S65141 Cr 2021 (print) | LCC PZ7.S65141 (ebook) | DDC [E]—dc23

The text of this book is set in 15.5-point Eames Century Modern, and Brandon Grotesque.
The illustrations were rendered digitally in Adobe Photoshop.
Book design by Rachael Cole

MANUFACTURED IN CHINA
10 9 8 7 6 5 4 3 2 1
First Edition

The CREATURE of HABIT

BY
JENNIFER E. SMITH

ILLUSTRATED BY
LEO ESPINOSA

RANDOM HOUSE STUDIO ▪ NEW YORK

On the island of Habit, there lived a creature.
He had very big teeth.
And very big eyes.
And very, very big feet.

Every day, the creature did the exact same things in the exact same order.

First, he ate three pineapples and two bananas.

Then he walked down to the water to say hello to the fish.

HELLO, FISH!

After that, he went looking for shells.

But he kept only the very best ones.

Next, he said hello to the trees.
HELLO, TREES!

And the rocks.
HELLO, ROCKS!

And the crab who lived under the rocks.
HELLO, CRAB!

When it was time for dinner, he ate three more pineapples and two more bananas.

Then he brushed his teeth and went to bed.
Every day was exactly the same. Which was
just how the creature liked it.

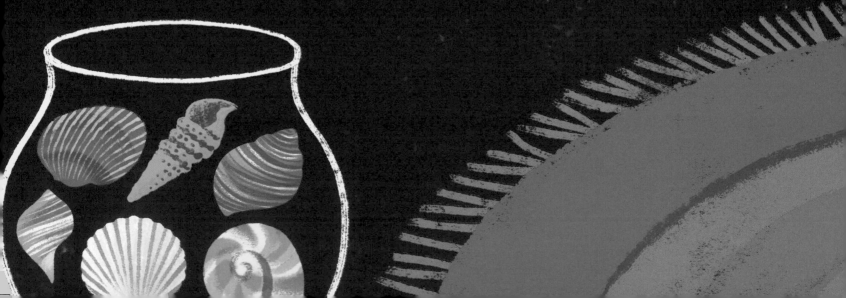

Then one morning, he spotted a boat.

It was a very small boat.

And it was carrying a very small creature.

He had very small teeth.

And very small eyes.

And very, very small feet.

Nobody had ever visited the island before, and the very big creature couldn't wait to show his new friend how everything worked.

He taught him how to collect pineapples and bananas and how to say hello to the fish.

HELLO, FISH!

HELLO, FISH!

He showed him how to find all the very best shells and when to eat his dinner and brush his teeth and go to bed.

The next morning, the very big creature woke up excited
to do it all over again. Just like he did every day.

But the very small creature was nowhere to be found.

When he finally appeared, he was excited to start the day, too.

Only instead of eating three pineapples and two bananas,
he ate a single coconut.

Instead of saying hello to the fish,

he went for a swim with them.

And instead of collecting shells,
he collected . . . well, everything else.

When it got dark, the very small creature didn't eat dinner or brush his teeth or go to bed. He just sat on the beach and looked at the stars.

Watching him, the very big creature's very big eye began to twitch.

This wasn't how things were done on the island of Habit. There was supposed to be a schedule. A routine. An order to things.

Otherwise, anything could happen.

For the next week, the very big creature kept an eye on the very small creature.

Some days the very small creature made sand castles after breakfast, and some days he stood on his head before dinner.

Some days he slept in,
and some days he stayed up late.

Some days he did nothing at all.

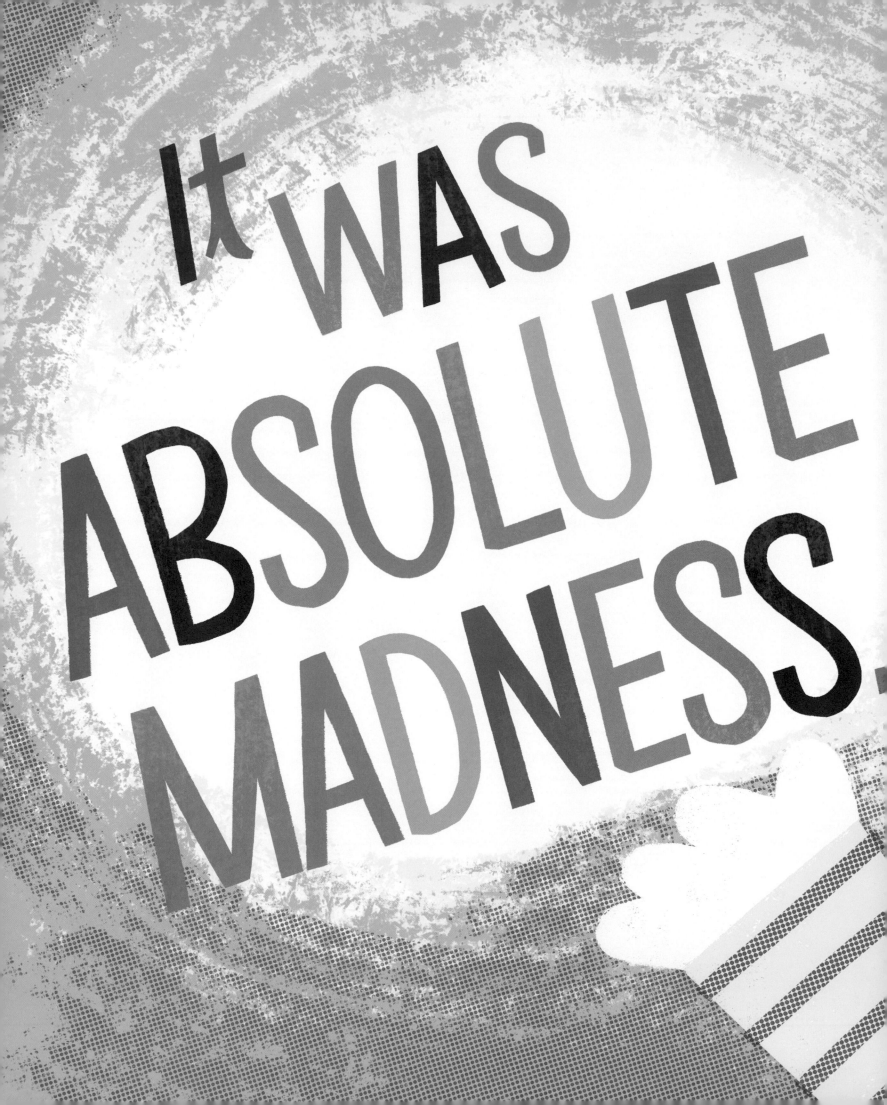

Then one morning, as the very big creature was eating his breakfast, the very small creature offered him an orange.

The very big creature looked at it carefully. It was smaller than a pineapple and rounder than a banana.

It was something he'd never tried before.

And it was . . . pretty good.

But not as good as a pineapple.

Afterward, he noticed the very small creature saying hello to the clouds.

The very big creature had said hello to a lot of things: the trees and the rocks and the crab who lived under the rocks. But never the clouds.

He thought about giving it a try. But he didn't want to miss his appointment with the fish.

Later, the very small creature found some treasures on the beach.

And even though he was meant to be looking for shells, the very big creature was secretly happy when he found a treasure, too.

The day was almost done. It was time to eat dinner and brush their teeth and go to bed. But the very small creature had other plans.

The very big creature watched him go, thinking about all the unusual things that had happened that day. The orange. And the clouds. And the treasures on the beach.

The very big creature sat down.

Then he stood up again,   his very big heart beating very, very fast.

Finally, he decided to follow the very small creature.

The very big creature had never been out at this hour before. Everything looked different. The sky was full of color, and the sun—as round as an orange—was disappearing into the water.

He knew this wasn't where he was supposed to be right now. But as the world turned from pink to orange to purple all around him, he wondered if maybe it actually was.

Later, they would eat dinner and brush
their teeth and go to bed.
    And tomorrow, there would be time to stick
to the schedule . . . if they wanted to.
    After all, anything could happen.
    But for now, the sky was beginning to
perform yet another magic trick.

Together, they sat and watched it change.